# MY LLAMA DRAMA

Lisa Keilma
2019 xx

For Max,
my little llama lover.
Keep laughing and
finding all the fun.

Created by Bear With Us Productions

Published by Brindie Books
Text and illustrations copyright © Lisa Kalma 2019

www.lisakalma.com

A catalogue record for this book is available from the National Library of Australia

ISBN 978 0 6484896 0 3 (hb)
ISBN 978 0 6484896 1 0 (pb)

# MY LLAMA DRAMA

Written by Lisa Kalma

Illustrated by Eduardo Paj

BEAR WITH US
PRODUCTIONS

# Oh, hi!

I'm glad you're here.

# I've got a problem.
# Lend an ear!

# You hear these llamas loudly munch?

They love their tasty
# hay at brunch.

But blow me down,
I swear it's true –

this llama said,

"You
want some
stew?"

You see, my llamas talk to me.
But talking llamas,

can that be?

They're chatting now.

I wouldn't lie. This fella burped then asked for pie.

One llama joked,
"I'll eat your hat!"

But joking llamas?
How 'bout that!

The baby asked,
"Are you my dad?"
That cutie's wrong.
I'm not a lad!

My herd of llamas speak to me.
**But speaking llamas,**
can that be?

Green Llama
asked me,
"Heads or tails?"

Black Llama
asked me,
"Paint my
nails?"

Pink Llama
said,
"I like
your hair."

White Llama
asked me,
"Truth
or dare?"

Blue Llama
said,
"I'll climb
this tree."

Grey Llama said,
"I'm a
bumble
bee!"

I'm sure I hear
a sing-along.
This llama's
rapping skills
are strong!

My herd of llamas sing to me.
But singing llamas,
can that be?

My ears aren't
bad or full of wax.

The tall
one said,
"My name is
Max."

Oh, can't you hear?
Oh, can't you see?
These llamas
really talk to me!
This craziness,
it must be true...

'cause I'm a talking llama too!

The llama is a long-necked animal native to South America.

Llamas are part of the camel family, but they don't have humps.

They are social animals and live with other llamas as a herd.

Although llamas are super smart and learn simple tasks quickly, they definitely cannot talk, chat, sing, dance, ask questions, or offer you stew...

## or can they?